Samuel French Acting Edition

The Thrush & The Woodpecker

by Steve Yockey

SAMUEL FRENCH

MUSIC USE NOTE

Licensees are solely responsible for obtaining formal written permission from copyright owners to use copyrighted music in the performance of this play and are strongly cautioned to do so. If no such permission is obtained by the licensee, then the licensee must use only original music that the licensee owns and controls. Licensees are solely responsible and liable for all music clearances and shall indemnify the copyright owners of the play(s) and their licensing agent, Concord Theatricals, against any costs, expenses, losses and liabilities arising from the use of music by licensees. Please contact the appropriate music licensing authority in your territory for the rights to any incidental music.

IMPORTANT BILLING AND CREDIT REQUIREMENTS

If you have obtained performance rights to this title, please refer to your licensing agreement for important billing and credit requirements.

THE THRUSH & THE WOODPECKER received a workshop production by the Source Festival in Washington, DC on June 19, 2014. The performance was directed by Cara Gabriel. The cast was as follows:

BRENDA HENDRIKS . . . . Alison Bauer

NOAH HENDRIKS . . . . .Alex Alferov

RÓISÍN DANNER . . . . Robin Covington

THE THRUSH & THE WOODPECKER was first produced by Actor's Express Theatre Company (Freddie Ashley, Artistic Director; Alex Scollon, Managing Director) in Atlanta, Georgia on October 31, 2015. It was directed by Melissa Foulger with sets by Kat Conley, costumes by Isabel A. Curley-Clay and Moriah Curley-Clay, lights by Ben Tilley, original music and sound by Haddon Kime, animations by Marisa Ginger Tontaveetong, and projections by Jon Summers. The production stage manager was Kristen Hennessy. The cast was as follows:

BRENDA HENDRIKS . . . . Stacy Melich

NOAH HENDRIKS . . . . .Matthew Busch

RÓISÍN DANNER . . . . Kathleen Wattis Kettrey

THE THRUSH & THE WOODPECKER additionally opened across the 2015-2016 season as a National New Play Network rolling world premiere at the following theaters: Kitchen Dog Theater (Dallas, TX) and The Custom Made Theatre Company (San Francisco, CA).

CHARACTERS

BRENDA HENDRIKS – a woman in her forties/fifties, fit, quick-witted & sharp-tongued but down to earth, practical, nurturing, and willing to roll up her sleeves

NOAH HENDRIKS – a young man, early twenties, something of a hipster idealist, sarcastic & sporting the worn charisma necessitated by a nomadic upbringing

RÓISÍN DANNER – a woman in her forties, stylish & graceful, her pleasant demeanor is an act masking rage; very put together, she commands a room with ease

AUTHOR'S NOTES

[ ] indicate overlapping dialogue.

The play takes place in the entry area and living room of a small house in the rolling hills and valleys of Northern California.

Shadow puppets are very smooth, bordering on filmic in execution. Perhaps even projections if possible. Realizing the immensity of their scale is the most important idea.

(Early morning. The living room of the **HENDRIKS'** *home. Small, well kept, comfortable. There is an entry area. The front door is visible.)*

*(***BRENDA*** *stands looking out the window. She is fit and casual in jeans and a simple, dark V-neck t-shirt. She has a scarf or bandana casually wrapped to hold her hair out of her face and a pair of gardening gloves jammed in her back pocket. She holds a mug of some kind. It seems casual, but she's lying in wait.)*

*(***NOAH*** *enters in pajama pants and t-shirt. Unsteady. He has a hipster vibe. He sees* ***BRENDA*** *and stops. Cautious. He looks like he might turn around. Instead he bucks up and crashes onto a chair. She glances at him then looks back out the window and sips from her mug.)*

NOAH. Is there coffee?

BRENDA. It's so early. Of course, you've been sleeping for over a day, I wondered if you'd ever wake up. You're just in time for the prettiest part of the morning. I have no idea why I thought east facing windows were so breathtaking; it gets too bright. It's something though, the light, you take it for granted; well not you, I mean me of course, but I was starting a bit of gardening and I thought, "Why don't you just stop for a moment and enjoy the morning?"

(She finally turns to him.)

And now you can enjoy it with me. Actually, I find it shocking that you were able to get any sleep at all. Not shocking, that's a bit much; I mean to say that I find it surprising that you weren't up all night trying to figure out what you're going to do with yourself now. In life I mean, rolling out before us, another [day dawning.]

NOAH. [You don't] [have to be so...]

BRENDA. [What do] people, people such as yourself, you'll have to forgive me, Noah, what do those people do when they're thrown out of an expensive private college after working so hard, after struggling so hard to get in? Imagine what would happen if someone like that were actually kicked out? Can you fathom it?

(Pause.)

I'm sure you can.

NOAH. That's my fault for asking about coffee.

BRENDA. Vandalism.

NOAH. You're saying it like, the way you say things.

BRENDA. I'm sorry, is there a positive way to say vandalism? Help me out here.

NOAH. It wasn't vandalism.

BRENDA. Breaking things, destroying things, a lot [of things.]

NOAH. [It wasn't] like that. Do you even want to know my side?

BRENDA. Not particularly.

NOAH. The administration refused, blithely even, dismissively, to make any changes to the outdoor lighting, even when I succinctly presented my written, my well-written and clearly documented grievances and I'm not going [to just...]

BRENDA. [Outdoor] lighting.

NOAH. Yes.

BRENDA. Pet project.

NOAH. Important issue.

BRENDA. Semantics.

NOAH. You know what? Don't. It's pollution.

BRENDA. I'm sorry, what was that?

NOAH. You heard me.

BRENDA. Have you perhaps taken my efforts to raise you with a green conscience to an entirely inexplicable, unproductive level?

NOAH. Is that a real question? It's a kind of pollution and should be acknowledged as such. With all of the money that school has to take corrective measures [they really...]

BRENDA. [When you say] outdoor lighting, I feel unprepared because you haven't shared your "grand manifesto" with me.

NOAH. Jesus.

BRENDA. So what encompasses "outdoor lighting"? You're talking about those tiny spotlights that illuminate signage, or street lamps, that kind of thing?

NOAH. It sounds small when you say it like that, but man-made light creates a kind of bubble that will eventually [inhibit...]

BRENDA. [So that's] a yes?

NOAH. Yes.

BRENDA. All right, am I listening to you? No, not anymore. I'm drinking this and enjoying the morning. Unless you're prepared to have an actual conversation, then please spare me these details and let me just drink this, whatever this is.

    (She drinks.)

NOAH. I need one guess.

BRENDA. Well if you only need one then it wouldn't be a guess, would it?

NOAH. That's fair.

BRENDA. Look at you. It's good to see you.

NOAH. It's good to see you too.

BRENDA. Have you been eating?

NOAH. Yes.

BRENDA. Just, you're thinner. And your hair.

NOAH. It's just messy right now.

BRENDA. Your hair. Your life. Everything.

NOAH. Okay, I walked into that one.

BRENDA. Didn't you.

NOAH. What did you do to my room?

BRENDA. Your room?

NOAH. That room. The room where I sleep that's suddenly full of books and a less than forgiving pull out couch.

BRENDA. Ah. Well, I foolishly thought that because you made it all the way to your senior year in college without being expelled for vandalism that making it one more year wouldn't be a problem, so Robert and I turned "your room" into a study. I apologize if the sleeper couch, the one that's meant for guests, isn't to your liking.

NOAH. I'll deal with it.

BRENDA. Temporarily.

NOAH. When's Robert coming back from Washington?

BRENDA. He can't.

NOAH. He can't?

BRENDA. He can't.

NOAH. He can't?

BRENDA. He can't. It's like a game, now you say it.

NOAH. Why can't he come back?

BRENDA. You're bright; reason it out.

NOAH. Okay. He can't come back from Washington because, okay, it's really early and I'm out of practice at talking with you, Mom.

(She toasts her mug to him.)

BRENDA. I raised you to be a thinker.

NOAH. And apparently you're in a bad mood.

BRENDA. And apparently you're a vandal.

NOAH. Stop it.

BRENDA. Hmmm, the topic is on my mind. If you'd rather discuss Robert at the moment then you'll have to reason it out.

NOAH. I don't know, I don't have enough to try to put together a plausible, okay, Robert can't come back from Washington because…you won't let him come back?

BRENDA. So wise. Always my fault.

NOAH. You've never been very good with men.

BRENDA. He can't come back from Washington because that's not where he is right now.

NOAH. I thought he was at Mt. Wilson?

BRENDA. Clearly.

NOAH. Look, he said he was going to Mt. Wilson in October.

BRENDA. He said a lot of things.

NOAH. Well then where is he?

BRENDA. Who knows, somewhere, he has to be somewhere. Let's get back to you.

NOAH. Mom, where's Robert?

BRENDA. He decided to go to Anchorage for a while. Something to do with a shipping deal, ostensibly, I didn't really ask. He has his own life.

NOAH. He's your husband.

BRENDA. Thank you.

NOAH. When's he coming back?

BRENDA. No idea. He might stay for a few extra days to "explore" the city. But trust me, he'll be more disappointed than I am, if possible, so if I were you I wouldn't be wishing for his return.

NOAH. Alaska, huh? I'm not surprised I guess. He loves the cold, so there he is. And you love the middle of nowhere, so here you are.

BRENDA. This is not the middle of nowhere; the highway is less than a mile down the drive. You're being hyperbolic, you're changing the subject, and you're doing a poor job of it.

NOAH. This is isolation.

BRENDA. This is space to breathe.

NOAH. Come on, we're always hidden away somewhere; it's always a project to get to wherever [we are.]

BRENDA. [Well you] don't live here anymore, so you don't have to deal with that.

NOAH. Think about how much happier we'd all be if we just lived somewhere beautiful, "tropically" beautiful, near water, on the beach. Somewhere like Hawaii.

BRENDA. You're being fanciful.

NOAH. I'm being absolutely serious.

BRENDA. It's a childish stalling tactic, but fine, for the sake of argument, let's say you actually mean that. You don't want to live in Hawaii, Noah. Robert's like old leather and I could probably handle it, but you with your pale skin, can you imagine? You're not made for the sun, like porcelain crisping red, just the thought of it. I took you to the beach [once...]

NOAH. [I definitely] remember.

BRENDA. You remember, and you, afraid of sharks, sunburned and all of your whining, and that's all I needed to know about you and the beach.

NOAH. I was a little boy.

BRENDA. You're still that little boy.

>   *(There is a quick, sharp knocking at the door.)*

NOAH. Thank god.

BRENDA. Are you expecting anyone?

NOAH. Maybe it's a rescue party.

BRENDA. You're definitely in need of rescue, but that's not an answer.

NOAH. No I'm not "expecting" anyone.

>   *(**NOAH** heads over and opens it. No one is there.)*

There's no one here.

(He looks around outside.)

BRENDA. Sometimes the woodpeckers attack the door.

NOAH. That sounded like a knock.

(He closes the door.)

BRENDA. It started recently. They like the wood. Or they don't like it. Either way, Robert says it's something about the particular wood we used.

NOAH. Isn't that bad for the door?

BRENDA. Undoubtedly. Here is another point to consider about your beach fantasy. There is an abundance of volcanic activity in Hawaii, volcanic instability. Over time, it breeds tentativeness. Besides, I've been and it isn't what you imagine, being there, being marooned in the Pacific.

NOAH. Good grief.

BRENDA. Never been a fan.

NOAH. Well, I don't think the people of Hawaii would share your assessment.

BRENDA. The indigenous people or the tourists who live there now?

NOAH. Tourists? Really Mom?

BRENDA. Of course the people of Hawaii would disagree, they're the "people of Hawaii." They don't know. You're born, you look around, ocean, ocean, ocean, you get used to how things are; that's how it works.

NOAH. Tell me about it.

(She puts down her drink.)

BRENDA. Oh, your life. So hard.

NOAH. I'm only saying that considering the number of times we moved before you met Robert and we actually settled in here, which is more than I can count or even remember, it would have been great to try somewhere like Hawaii. That's the only point I was making.

BRENDA. Well, I'm happy here. That's why I wasn't going to go to Washington with Robert in the first place and it's why I'm not wrapped up in a parka in Alaska right now.

NOAH. He asked you to go?

BRENDA. Who can say?

NOAH. You can say.

BRENDA. He usually asks me to go. But it's a good thing I didn't go or else who would be here to welcome you.

NOAH. You should have gone. It's not good for you to spend so much time alone.

BRENDA. That garden takes a lot of work.

NOAH. I worry about you.

BRENDA. I love you, but don't push it.

NOAH. Why didn't you go?

BRENDA. He doesn't notice the difference and we just... needed a bit of time apart, don't make that face, apart from each other. Everything is fine.

NOAH. Mom.

BRENDA. He wants some time to think about things, all right?

NOAH. What things?

BRENDA. Noah, when I use a word as general as "things" it's because I'm not going to tell you anything more specific beyond the word itself. That's between the two of us and nothing for you to worry about. You certainly have your own concerns at the moment and you never even liked Robert anyway.

NOAH. He's a territorial jerk but I like that you like him and I like that he makes you happy. So don't talk like he's gone if you don't know for sure that he's gone.

BRENDA. I've never been very good with men; you said that.

NOAH. You should have told me something was wrong.

BRENDA. There's nothing to tell. Yet.

NOAH. Is he leaving?

BRENDA. That's not what I said and I know you were listening.

NOAH. If he leaves, are you going to [have to...]

BRENDA. [Don't get] ahead of yourself.

NOAH. Will you have to go back to work?

BRENDA. Excuse me, I have a job.

NOAH. Volunteer work at the library is not a job; it's volunteer work.

BRENDA. It's distasteful to look down your nose at things, Noah. And the money from leasing the land is more than sufficient.

NOAH. Whoa, will you even get to keep the land, the house? He's the [one that...]

BRENDA. [Look at] me. Nothing's happened yet, so how can I answer you? Robert is a good man and we needed some space. I shouldn't need to explain it twice and I will not explain it again.

NOAH. Did he go to Alaska by himself?

BRENDA. And I'm here by myself. Except for you. Unexpected.

NOAH. For both of us.

BRENDA. Couldn't behave.

NOAH. Are you drinking whatever that is because of Robert?

BRENDA. Jesus Christ, if I wasn't standing here to, you listen to me, seldom do I use this tone with you, young man, because you're smarter than it implies. I've spent a good deal of time alone in my life and it's much better to have people around you. So clearly I'm not happy about this situation with Robert, but I'm doing my best not to indulge in any anxiety I might be experiencing. And I will not have you using my personal life as a tangential escape route to avoid me; it's petty.

NOAH. That's not [what I'm...]

BRENDA. [And even if] you're actually concerned, thank you for that, it just makes your pressing on the topic now opportunistic. I got a room ready, I made you soup, I've let you recover a bit from something that

I'm sure was difficult and hurt your pride, but what you've done is serious, the repercussions are serious. You make grown up choices and you have to take the grown up consequences so please give me some small glimmer that you understand that basic fundamental even a little because it would at least be a place to start.

(*Pause.*)

NOAH. I'm sorry.

(*She throws her hands up and picks up her mug again as if she might really just walk out of the room.*)

BRENDA. Ugh, that's such an easy thing to say when confronted with your actions. Don't be sorry, don't regret things, be able to defend them. To yourself. And to me.

NOAH. Look, just, do you want me to leave?

(*She spins on her heel, diving right back into the thick of it.*)

BRENDA. Ah, okay, where would you go?

NOAH. I don't know.

BRENDA. Then it's another empty thing to say.

NOAH. Mom, it wasn't vandalism.

BRENDA. Smashing the campus streetlamps and any other outdoor lights [you could find.]

NOAH. [I'm trying to explain] how all of this unnecessary, man-made illumination is blocking [out the...]

BRENDA. [Save the] activist stump speech, please.

NOAH. It's not just a talking point, I'm studying astronomy.

BRENDA. Not anymore.

NOAH. It's too important to me, to what I hope to do, [to observe...]

BRENDA. [You're] getting closer.

NOAH. Jesus, what do you want to hear?

BRENDA. Why did you do it? You, specifically, Noah, why did [you do it?]

NOAH. [I was doing] what I thought was right!

> *(She stops, cocks her head and grins.)*

What?

BRENDA. Now, that is an answer.

NOAH. Okay, good.

BRENDA. You were doing what you thought was right.

NOAH. Yes.

BRENDA. In the dark. With a hammer.

NOAH. Yes.

BRENDA. All right, let me just…an evil man-made "bubble" of light is going to blot out the night sky, rendering the stars invisible, isolating us from the rest of the galaxy, blinding us from the bigger picture.

NOAH. We learned about it in my optics class and there are [very real…]

BRENDA. [So as a] whole, we'll eventually lose our ability to see the stars but also our perspective on our place in things. Something like that?

NOAH. I thought you hadn't read my manifesto?

BRENDA. I read National Geographic. And I'm the one that showed you all of those constellations when you were little, so please don't act like I'm ignorant. Now, you don't really have a manifesto, do you? You haven't gone that far down the road towards idealistic self-destruction?

NOAH. Not per se.

BRENDA. You acted on your beliefs.

NOAH. Yes. And I would fully think you'd support that.

BRENDA. Really?

NOAH. Yes.

BRENDA. You'd still think that, really?

NOAH. Yes I would and do think that, in fact, yes.

BRENDA. You'll be unsurprised when I admit to not knowing everything. I suspect you've thought that for quite some time. But I do know what it is to make a decision that seems questionable. I know what it means to choose the unconventional for the sake of what seems right.

NOAH. "Seems" right?

BRENDA. Or what we think is right, Noah, but everyone has different ideas about what that means. So I'm telling you right now I can understand. And I hope you can understand how important it is to me for you to achieve something, for you to be able to hold your head high [and…]

NOAH. [Why?]

BRENDA. Because I'm your mother and if you need a better reason: so you can have some semblance of a happy life.

NOAH. You're blowing this way out of proportion, it's not like my whole life [is going…]

BRENDA. [Noah, my issue] with you is nothing grand or philosophical. It's simpler and much more personal.

NOAH. Okay.

BRENDA. After everything you've been through, after having to grow up with me as a mother, like this, forced to think, forced to understand, I still don't think you sat down before you did this and weighed the cost of causing all of that damage; the actual cost. You were angry and felt marginalized, so you acted from a place of embarrassment and desperately hoped that you wouldn't get caught.

NOAH. No, I didn't even think about it, I didn't care about getting caught, this [is so…]

> (**BRENDA** *leans forward and places the mug down again forcefully.*)

BRENDA. [That's not] a better answer; please don't sound so proud when you brag about not thinking. You have to stand up for what you believe in, absolutely, but you also always have to understand what you're giving up.

NOAH. I did.

BRENDA. No more school in exchange for breaking easily replaceable lighting fixtures.

NOAH. Yes!

BRENDA. That were probably up and running again by last night.

NOAH. It was worth it!

BRENDA. I find that hard to believe.

NOAH. Believe it or don't, it doesn't make a difference now, does it? Here I am. But it was the right thing. And I do feel bad about it, okay? It's not like I'm proud of myself for fucking the whole thing up, but you did raise me to stand up for what I believe in and if you can't see that's what I was doing then maybe you're just not looking hard enough, not even trying to understand, and all I wanted was some fucking coffee, I just came out here to ask about coffee, god, which I can just make for myself, all right?

> *(Pause.)*

BRENDA. You'll make it yourself?

NOAH. What?

BRENDA. You'll make the coffee yourself? That would be something, wouldn't that be something?

NOAH. I can make coffee.

BRENDA. No doubt.

NOAH. Okay, you know what? I make excellent coffee.

BRENDA. Huh. All right then, let me just say, because it seems clear you need to hear it: I'm so proud, you know? I've worked so hard, supporting you, keeping you on track and to see you here now, ready to make your own coffee, I don't know if you're aware, but I'm so very, exceptionally proud of you.

> *(Pause. Stand off. He eventually drops his gaze. She picks up her mug again.)*

I know you want me to let you off the hook, but clearly that's not how this is going to play out. So let's get past the sparring portion, even though it's such fantastic sport, and figure out what you're going to do now.

NOAH. Fine.

> *(She rises to leave. As she passes him, she stops and lifts his face to look at her.)*

BRENDA. You know that I love you.

NOAH. Yes.

BRENDA. Just so we're on the same page.

NOAH. Yes.

> *(She places her hand on his shoulder. He puts his hand on top of hers and gives it a squeeze.)*

BRENDA. Good. I need to splash some water on my face and then run into town quickly, so you'll have some time to formulate a new game plan while I'm gone. But when I get back, we're having a talk about this, about you, about exactly how long you'll be sleeping on that sofa bed and what's next for you, got it?

NOAH. Yes.

BRENDA. That's a start.

> *(She exits. He sulks.)*

NOAH. *(Quietly.)* Good to be home. Love you too.

BRENDA. *(From offstage.)* I hope you're not pretending that this reaction is anything unexpected, anything that you couldn't have foreseen when you decided to start smashing other people's property under cover of night.

NOAH. Uh huh.

BRENDA. *(From offstage.)* That's not a reply, that's just a guttural noise.

NOAH. Uh huh.

> *(There is another quick, sharp knocking at the door. **NOAH** heads over and opens it. No one is there. He looks around outside and closes the door.)*

BRENDA. *(From offstage.)* Is that the door?

NOAH. No.

> *(**BRENDA** enters looking refreshed, she is finishing the last of her drink.)*

BRENDA. Woodpeckers.

> *(She hands him the mug as she passes him. He smells it.)*

NOAH. I guessed right on the drink.

BRENDA. Congratulations.

NOAH. So...it's a little bit early for whiskey.

> *(***BRENDA*** *looks through her purse.)*

BRENDA. It's not "whiskey." It's coffee with a splash of whiskey and you're in no position at the moment to lecture me about anything.

NOAH. So it's a little bit early for whiskey.

BRENDA. Do you feel better now? I can't find my keys.

NOAH. They're probably over on the table by the door.

BRENDA. Ah.

> *(Crossing to the table, she stops and looks him up and down.)*

NOAH. What?

BRENDA. Nothing.

> *(She continues to stand still, looking at him.)*

NOAH. What? I'm sorry I got kicked out of that stupid, elitist college, okay? I said I was sorry and I meant it even though that's not how you want [to hear it.]

BRENDA. [I'm just looking] at you and wondering: do you think you'll be cleaning yourself up today?

NOAH. Jesus, I didn't even have any coffee yet.

BRENDA. All right.

NOAH. Thank you.

BRENDA. So then you will be cleaning yourself up today?

NOAH. I'll do my level best.

BRENDA. That's a bit subjective lately, isn't it?

NOAH. Clearly.

> *(***BRENDA*** *grabs the keys.* ***NOAH*** *exits in a huff toward his bedroom.)*

BRENDA. I'll be back soon. And then we talk.

> *(She exits.)*

> *(After a moment, there is a knocking at the door. This time it is a more familiar sound.* **NOAH** *comes back in fastening jeans. He is still barefoot and unshowered as he heads towards the door.)*

NOAH. I'm going to permanently attach house keys to your wrist if you can't...

> *(He opens the door to find* **RÓISÍN**. *She is in a silk blouse or thin, fitted sweater, slacks, high-heel boots, perhaps a jacket. She is adjusting a beautiful scarf around her neck. She has a large clutch. Everything about her speaks of careful planning. As the door opens, there is the sound of birds scattering.* **RÓISÍN** *looks over her shoulder towards the sound, apparently a bit startled.)*

RÓISÍN. So many birds.

NOAH. Oh, sorry. I thought you were my Mom. She's always forgetting her, you know, it doesn't matter. Sorry.

> *(She looks him up and down.)*

RÓISÍN. Not at all.

NOAH. Can I help you?

RÓISÍN. I'm looking for Brenda Hendriks?

NOAH. She's not here right now.

RÓISÍN. Ah. Hmm. Did you see all of those birds?

NOAH. No.

RÓISÍN. All over the lawn.

NOAH. Where?

RÓISÍN. You scared them away. The door, I mean. But there were so many.

NOAH. Huh. You were, you're here to see my Mom?

RÓISÍN. You can't possibly be Brenda's son?

NOAH. I'm Noah. Nice to meet you.

RÓISÍN. All right.

NOAH. She just ran into town for a minute, was she expecting you?

RÓISÍN. Probably not.

NOAH. Happy to tell her you stopped by if, I'm sorry, what was your name?

RÓISÍN. Róisín Danner.

NOAH. Are you staying in town?

RÓISÍN. Do you mind if I wait?

NOAH. In here?

RÓISÍN. You're right; I'll just come back. But it's quite an undertaking getting out here.

NOAH. Yes it is. No, I mean, it's fine. Come in, please. We don't have guests very often, so I'm just a little rusty. Of course it's all right.

> (**RÓISÍN** *enters and takes in the room. She sets down her clutch and scarf.*)

RÓISÍN. I appreciate it, really.

NOAH. Make yourself at home.

RÓISÍN. Huh, this place looks like your Mom. Looks like the way I remember her. Does that make sense?

NOAH. I think so.

RÓISÍN. It just takes me back.

NOAH. Can I get you anything?

RÓISÍN. Do you have any Scotch? I take it neat.

> (**NOAH** *begins to exit.* **RÓISÍN** *looks at him blankly before holding up her hand...*)

Are you, are you really going to get me Scotch?

NOAH. If I can find some, sure. I don't know if there's any in the house [right now.]

RÓISÍN. [That's, huh,] very accommodating of you.

NOAH. Okay.

RÓISÍN. Do you often have guests in the early morning asking for Scotch?

NOAH. I think I mentioned we don't really ever have guests. And you asked for Scotch.

(*She laughs at him, a small thing.*)

RÓISÍN. Yes, I remember that.

NOAH. So you weren't serious?

RÓISÍN. No. I don't need any Scotch. That was apparently a very poor joke on my part. But I appreciate the hospitality and some hot tea would be wonderful.

NOAH. Tea.

RÓISÍN. Please.

NOAH. I can do that. But are you sure this time? Because I'm going to go in there and make some tea for you now.

(**RÓISÍN** *smiles at him and nods.*)

It'll take a minute for the water.

RÓISÍN. I don't mind.

(**NOAH** *exits.*)

(*As soon as he leaves the room,* **RÓISÍN** *leans against a chair for support, almost overcome. She clutches at her stomach and looks as if she may weep. She looks up taking in a huge breath and tries to compose herself, suddenly doubling over again.* **NOAH** *enters.*)

NOAH. Like I said, it'll only be a minute for the...

(*She jerks upright as he enters.*)

Are you okay?

RÓISÍN. Oh, yes, don't give it a thought, my back is just twisted into knots from the trip. I don't know what it will take to sort it out at this point.

NOAH. Do you need to sit down?

RÓISÍN. I'm fine, thank you for asking.

NOAH. You just got in?

RÓISÍN. Yes. Long flight.

NOAH. From where?

RÓISÍN. Boston. Actually just north.

NOAH. I've never been on an airplane, believe it or not.

RÓISÍN. That's unusual.

NOAH. We drive everywhere.

RÓISÍN. Car people?

NOAH. That's a good way to say it.

RÓISÍN. How would you say it?

NOAH. Nomadic.

RÓISÍN. Hmm. I don't have much use for airplanes so I won't try to change your mind.

NOAH. You don't like them?

RÓISÍN. As it happens, I don't.

NOAH. Got you here in one piece though.

RÓISÍN. Did I say I took a plane?

NOAH. *(With a chuckle.)* You said it was a long flight.

RÓISÍN. Stick to the roads.

> *(She winks.)*

NOAH. Okay. I'm sure if my Mom knew then she could have been here to meet you.

RÓISÍN. Do you think?

NOAH. It's just with guests, you know? She usually makes a big production out of it.

RÓISÍN. Honestly, it's been a while and I just thought I'd surprise her. Maybe that was a bad idea, but it's what I decided to do and here I am.

NOAH. No, it's fine. It's great actually, I was just telling her that she spends too much time out here without, huh, it's just nice she'll have some company.

RÓISÍN. Good. And it's been a long time coming.

> *(The whistle of the teapot sounds.)*

NOAH. Right back.

>*(He slips away to get the tea. **RÓISÍN** walks towards the front door and then quickly spins around, taking in the room.)*

RÓISÍN. Bitch.

NOAH. *(From offstage.)* Milk or sugar?

RÓISÍN. Both, thank you.

>*(She opens and closes her hand making a fist. Bracing. As **NOAH** comes back into the room with a mug, she pulls herself together, pleasant demeanor restored. He hands her the mug.)*

NOAH. Here you go.

RÓISÍN. Thank you very much.

NOAH. Probably better let it cool for a minute.

RÓISÍN. I forgot to ask this: on my way in I noticed the, I'm embarrassed to say I don't know what they're properly called in this incarnation? Windmills?

NOAH. Oh, the wind turbines? Sure.

RÓISÍN. They're beautiful. Rows and rows of them, I've never seen anything like it.

NOAH. I love to just stare at them sometimes. It's hypnotic.

RÓISÍN. And they're immense.

NOAH. They look bigger than they actually are, from far away I mean.

RÓISÍN. Do they belong to you?

NOAH. We lease the land to an alternative energy start-up and sort of keep an eye on them. Actually, they have people for that, we don't officially watch them. It's not like someone could just walk away with one or anything; like you said, they're pretty big. The hills on our property, Robert's property, they're ideal for it though. So the company came in and built them. It's something else.

RÓISÍN. Robert? Is that your father?

NOAH. He's my mother's husband.

RÓISÍN. Ah, thus the use of the first name. Where's your father?

NOAH. Uh, was it Mrs. Danner?

RÓISÍN. Ms. Danner.

NOAH. I'm sure my Mom will be back soon.

RÓISÍN. Oh no, I'm asking too many questions. I do that, I'm aware of it and I just can't stop myself. I'm always so curious about other people's lives. Why they do the things they do, how they get to where they are, choices, like that. I apologize.

NOAH. No, I didn't mean to, this is the longest conversation I've had with anyone in a while. Except my Mom and those aren't really conversations, so...

> *(He shrugs. She inhales deeply from the mug. She then looks at the mug, smiles and looks at* **NOAH.***)*

RÓISÍN. Maple?

NOAH. I'm impressed, most people can't tell from the smell.

RÓISÍN. Ah, I'm not most people, Noah. I'll say it's an interesting choice and it smells wonderful.

NOAH. Just tell my Mom I was a good host. Please. Or I'll never hear the end of it.

RÓISÍN. You've been an excellent host.

NOAH. That will relieve her some. She's not very happy with me right now. Actually, your visit might take the heat off of me a little, so great timing all around.

RÓISÍN. What did you do? That's another question, I know, but it seems like a logical progression [from your...]

NOAH. [I don't] mind. Vandalism. That's what she'll tell you, I'm sure. We're currently finding some common ground to talk about it.

RÓISÍN. To talk about it.

NOAH. Yep.

RÓISÍN. Vandalism. Isn't that something? Hopefully she smacked you around a little bit. Huh, I don't mind telling you that's what I would do.

NOAH. She did.

RÓISÍN. Good for her.

NOAH. She just doesn't understand; I take this seriously. If I want to really be able to pursue a career in astronomy, light pollution matters.

RÓISÍN. All right, that brings any number of questions to mind, but I'm trying to be on my best behavior now.

NOAH. No, please go ahead.

RÓISÍN. Well in no particular order, what is light pollution? Is astronomy something someone can have a career in? And why would you choose such an unconventional field?

NOAH. Is it unconventional?

RÓISÍN. Only in so much as I've never met an astronomer, but that probably shouldn't be the recognized standard of what's conventional.

NOAH. All right, let me just, I'll just keep this simple.

RÓISÍN. I'm actually pretty sharp.

NOAH. I'll keep it simple so that I don't end up talking for two days.

RÓISÍN. Ah, thanks for that.

NOAH. Light pollution, very generally, is the impact that man made illumination has on our ability to see the night sky, the stars. It's a problem, a growing problem. Especially for astronomers. Or mostly for astronomers, at this point, and that's what I'm trying, was trying to become.

RÓISÍN. Why astronomy?

NOAH. I mentioned we moved around a lot?

RÓISÍN. Nomadic.

NOAH. No matter where we lived, I could always find the same stars. Well, in this hemisphere anyway. That's incredibly reductive, but I guess the night sky has always been a comfort. That's maybe a big part of how all of this started.

RÓISÍN. That is an absolutely lovely explanation.

NOAH. I'm over-romanticizing.

RÓISÍN. There's nothing wrong with that, nothing at all. Astronomy lets you study the stars, study what you love.

NOAH. Not just stars, it's basically focusing on any celestial objects, anything that's outside of us, outside of the Earth's atmosphere.

RÓISÍN. Far away things. Things you'll never touch.

NOAH. I've...huh, I've never thought of it that way.

RÓISÍN. Probably not the best way to think about it.

NOAH. Food for thought.

> *(He smiles and nods. **RÓISÍN** sits gently on the edge of the couch. It's more like perching. She sips her tea and stares at **NOAH**. He smiles. She smiles. He takes a stroll around the room. She follows him with her eyes.)*

RÓISÍN. Compared to most trips to town, is this a particularly long one?

NOAH. She shouldn't be much longer. So, did you two go to school together or [something?]

RÓISÍN. [I'm just now] taking the time to notice. You're a very attractive young man.

NOAH. Uh...

RÓISÍN. I hope that doesn't, I'm not propositioning you.

NOAH. No, I didn't think that.

RÓISÍN. Good.

NOAH. Yes.

RÓISÍN. But you are very attractive.

NOAH. Okay, thanks.

RÓISÍN. You know that though, don't you? You seem like maybe you know that.

NOAH. Um, I'm not really sure how to answer that.

RÓISÍN. Honestly.

NOAH. I look normal, I guess.

RÓISÍN. It's striking to me. How old are you?

(**NOAH** *puffs up a bit.*)

NOAH. How old do you think?

RÓISÍN. How old do I think?

NOAH. How old do you think?

RÓISÍN. I'm asking you.

NOAH. No, I want you to guess. People always guess [older.]

RÓISÍN. [Let's not] do that, I've never experienced that game ending well.

NOAH. I'm twenty-two.

RÓISÍN. Huh, your mother and I weren't much older than that when we last saw each other. Well, a few years at that age makes a huge difference.

(*The punctuated knocking sounds again at the front door.* **RÓISÍN** *stands up.* **NOAH** *doesn't really acknowledge it.*)

NOAH. So how exactly do you know my Mom?

RÓISÍN. Are you going to answer the door?

NOAH. No, it's fine.

RÓISÍN. Are you sure?

NOAH. Woodpeckers. I said that like I know, really it's just something Mom told me about this morning. I haven't been around much lately, but apparently they've started attacking the door recently. Not attacking, pecking at or whatever you call what they do.

RÓISÍN. Drumming. It's called drumming.

NOAH. Huh. It has something to do with the wood.

RÓISÍN. Or they're just trying to get in.

NOAH. Or that.

RÓISÍN. It's funny, not funny, but I have something of a history with woodpeckers.

NOAH. Seriously?

RÓISÍN. Oh yes. I realize it's an odd thing. You've only just met me and I've certainly been giving you the third degree without sharing very much about myself. But it's uncanny that those particular birds would come up while we're sitting here waiting. There's a story if you're interested? Hmm, if you're not too afraid when someone old enough to be your mother says, "There's a story."

NOAH. Not afraid. Oh, do you need some more hot water?

RÓISÍN. No thank you, this is fine.

NOAH. So tell me about your "something of a history with woodpeckers."

RÓISÍN. That's just what I said; you pay close attention.

NOAH. Kind of a must in this house. You know Mom.

(She smiles and sips her tea, sitting down at a small table. She takes note of a framed photo of **BRENDA** *and* **NOAH.***)*

RÓISÍN. Hmm.

NOAH. You were saying…?

RÓISÍN. Yes?

NOAH. The story.

(She sets down her mug.)

RÓISÍN. Yes, absolutely. Well, this was so long ago now, I was much younger, where to begin. There was a woman who lived in my town. She had been going through a particularly difficult time. That's generous; she wasn't in a good place at all.

NOAH. What happened?

RÓISÍN. It's not important.

NOAH. Doesn't it kind of set the stage?

RÓISÍN. No one ever really talked about the details. People rarely care about the finer points. But she had, her husband left her suddenly and then there was a series of rather tragic events. And loss. Does that work for you?

NOAH. Sure.

RÓISÍN. Needless to say she was something of a wreck. More of a walking corpse, truth be told. It's embarrassing to remember her that way. The only time she left her

house was to walk out to the mailbox each afternoon.
I used to watch her. Bathrobe, slippers, probably exactly
what you imagine if you were to imagine the cliché of
a woman coming undone. Although she wasn't crying,
I never saw her cry, so maybe not exactly what you'd
imagine, but you get the idea.

> *(One entire wall of the living room begins
> to glow, warm, becoming an opaque screen.
> A shadow representation of a small row of
> houses appears in the distance. A shadow of a
> woman appears on the screen and she makes
> her way to the mailbox.)*

One afternoon she came across something lying in the
driveway. It was a woodpecker, a male bird. The red
head gives it away, you know? The females have black
heads, but the males are more colorful. She bought
a book on the subject. I never saw the book, so it's
perhaps only a convenience to add detail. But from that
book, she learned this was an Ivory Billed Woodpecker
and that this particular bird could grow to have a
wingspan of up to three feet. That seems, well at the
time it must have been unimaginable. This poor little
bird was on death's door after all and it fit in the palm
of her hand, just like this.

> *(She gently holds out her cupped hand as
> the shadow figure kneels down and picks up
> something off the ground.)*

NOAH. Small.

RÓISÍN. Yes, so small.

NOAH. Too small?

RÓISÍN. How do you mean?

NOAH. Did it die?

> *(She stops, leans one elbow on the table
> and smiles at him. As the shadow woman
> disappears from view.)*

RÓISÍN. And here I thought you were a good listener?

NOAH. Sorry.

> *(The houses fade as a table appears in shadow. A grandfather clock sits in the background with its pendulum bob swaying rhythmically. A small box sits on the table. The woman crosses to the box and places the bird inside it.)*

RÓISÍN. So this broken woman took the bird in and made a little nest for it inside an old shoebox. Makeshift at best, you can imagine. It would just lie there, eyes wide open, and stare at her. She would bring it bits of fruit, a thimble of water. Not just the common sense things though. She also offered up everything she felt to the injured bird. The few good things, the many bad, those feelings you have for just a flash of a moment and then regret having for days on end after; she took all of them and poured them into this bird. Everything. Everything. And time passed.

> *(The shadow woman gently touches the box and then exits.)*

Much to her surprise, the bird got better. Now, it was hard for her to tell at first with no particular training in ornithology. But she woke up each morning expecting to find him dead inside the box and each morning he was still there, waiting for her, staring at her. With these bottomless eyes.

> *(The hands on the clock face begin to move faster, but the pendulum bob stays at the same rate. The sound of a woodpecker call, softly, almost inaudible begins to rise from the box on the table.)*

Then after more time, he started greeting her each morning with a quiet chirping, something of a fledgling call.

> *(The shadow woman returns to the table. She places her hand over her heart as she leans on

*the table looking into the box. The bird hops
up and down a bit in the box popping into
view.)*

And then after more time, up on his feet, with a
tentative shake of the wing here and there. After more
time, he took to flying. Still waiting patiently each
morning for the woman to wake up and check in on
him, but flying around the house.

*(The hands on the clock face move even faster
as the bird flutters out of the box and around
above the shadow woman. She claps and lifts
her hands as if she might try to join him.)*

She was delighted in a way that she had thought gone
forever. Sometimes she would even smile, this broken
woman. And the bird grew.

*(The clock hands spin and spin. A larger bird
appears fluttering above her.)*

And, although it seemed almost unthinkable, he grew
even more.

*(An even larger bird appears. The shadow
woman reaches her hand up and genuinely
tries to touch the fluttering bird.)*

And he kept growing until it seemed he never could
have fit into the palm of her hand. This beautiful bird,
beautiful even in fits of excitement or rage, had once
been just a day away from death. And she decided
that the bird's miraculous recovery was a sign from
some higher power. I won't pretend to name it here;
I wouldn't even venture a guess. But it was a sign. And
so she pulled herself up and began the arduous process
of reclaiming her life.

*(The lights return to normal and the shadows
fade.)*

I editorialized the ending a bit, to be honest. But I like
that ending.

NOAH. What happened to the woodpecker?

RÓISÍN. Ah, you're more interested in the fate of the wounded bird than the broken woman? It's not really an epilogue kind of story.

NOAH. Epilogues aren't in your wheelhouse?

> (**RÓISÍN** *smiles at him. The lights dim as the wall is illuminated again. An empty chair is present.*)

RÓISÍN. All right then. At a certain point, and this was after a long while, at least a few years, it became impractical to keep him in the house. This large bird flying around, and as he got healthier he got more rambunctious.

> (*The shadow of the woman enters and sits in the chair. It closely echoes* **RÓISÍN***'s current position. The grandfather clock has stopped. There is no movement. It is broken. It is cracked.*)

That's not embellishment. I'm not ascribing the bird human qualities as a narrative device for your benefit.

> (*The loud sound of wings flapping, stirring, causes the shadow woman to look up at a sharp angle. Everything on the screen shakes. The grandfather clock falls over. She stands up.*)

He actually became this kind of effervescent force, breaking things, slamming around; once he got started there was nothing to be done. And if the bird were to get angry, well, the damage was simply beyond belief. So as much as it pained the woman, she had to set the bird free. And that's just what she did.

> (*The shadow of a woodpecker eclipses a huge portion of the wall and causes the shadow woman to fall back. This is only seen for a moment and then, almost as quickly, the wall images disappear.*)

But I'll tell you, that woodpecker wouldn't leave; it stayed on with her for years. Hidden, full of everything that woman ever was and ever would be ever again.

> (*A deafening bird cry rips through the space.* **NOAH** *jumps up and* **RÓISÍN** *places her hand over her heart, startled.*)

NOAH. What the fuck!?!

RÓISÍN. So loud.

> (**NOAH** *rushes to the front door and throws it open. The sound of dozens of birds scattering rushes in as* **NOAH** *looks in both directions.*)

NOAH. I saw all of the birds you were talking about. They scattered again, but there were so many. They can't all be woodpeckers; do woodpeckers travel in flocks?

> (*He closes the door.*)

RÓISÍN. It's called a "descent."

NOAH. What?

RÓISÍN. When a group of woodpeckers is gathered like that. It's not a flock; it's a descent.

NOAH. That seems like an intentionally ominous thing to call it. I've never seen more than one or two at a time.

RÓISÍN. They must really have something to say.

NOAH. Well, that's a creepy thought. There's never anything that loud out here. Ever.

RÓISÍN. Ever? Really though, there are so many little things every day that would simply baffle us if we tried to explain them away. Don't you find? Or that might just be my experience. Could I trouble you for some more hot water?

NOAH. What? Oh, of course. Yes. I think I just got a little caught up in your story.

> (**NOAH** *heads over and takes the mug from* **RÓISÍN.**)

RÓISÍN. I doubt very seriously that we just heard a giant woodpecker.

NOAH. Can you imagine?

RÓISÍN. I wouldn't even know where to start.

NOAH. I'll be right back.

>   *(He exits. **RÓISÍN** is immediately up. She moves to the window and looks outside, more accurately she looks up into the sky.)*

>   *(She grabs a small notebook or scrap of paper and a pen from a nearby shelf then returns to the chair. She begins anxiously humming a tune* as she writes something on one of the pages, tears it out and folds it in half as **NOAH** returns. She is still humming as she pockets the folded piece of paper.)*

RÓISÍN. Hope you don't mind, just needed to jot something down.

NOAH. Huh, I know that song you were humming. Maybe.

RÓISÍN. Not a common song.

>   *(She begins again and after a moment he picks up humming along with her. This lasts for a moment. As they finish the phrase, **NOAH** seems confused.)*

It's a beautiful tune, isn't it? It always reminds me of a thrush song. The way it meanders.

NOAH. A thrush is a bird, right? Another bird story?

RÓISÍN. No, I'm afraid not.

NOAH. Are you sure?

RÓISÍN. Yes, yes. We only had one wreck of a woman in our town to tell stories about.

NOAH. But she pulled it together in the end.

RÓISÍN. At least in the version you heard.

NOAH. I'll just pretend it worked out for her.

---

*A license to produce *The Thrush & The Woodpecker* does not include a performance license for any third-party or copyrighted music. Licensees should create an original composition or use music in the public domain. For further information, please see Music Use Note on page 3.

RÓISÍN. Do that. And as much as I'm sure you're just dying to sit through another one of my lengthy stories, I don't have any more and certainly nothing about a thrush.

NOAH. Or even a flock of thrush.

RÓISÍN. A "mutation" of thrush.

NOAH. Not really? Who would name a group of anything a "mutation"?

RÓISÍN. And yet, that is what it's called.

NOAH. I'm not sure I believe you.

RÓISÍN. Regardless, there is no thrush story. It's just the impression the tune of the song gives me, that's all. This cup of tea gets you one woodpecker story, one thrush song, and one grateful unexpected guest.

NOAH. What was that song?

RÓISÍN. Something my mother used to sing to me. Honestly, I don't even remember her singing it, but I still remember the song.

> *(The punctuated knocking sounds again. This time from multiple sources against the door, different rhythms and tenors but all quick and sharp.)*

The birds are back?

> *(Suddenly the knocking stops, the sounds of birds scattering as the door opens and* **BRENDA** *swings into the house already speaking. She closes the door behind her, removing sunglasses.)*

BRENDA. Jesus, did you see all of those birds outside? They were practically organizing a full-scale assault on the front door, I've never seen [anything like...]

NOAH. [Mom, Mom] you have a visitor.

BRENDA. What do you mean? I didn't...

> *(**RÓISÍN** stands. **BRENDA** stops. She drops her sunglasses.)*

RÓISÍN. Here you are.

NOAH. Mom? Mrs. Danner's been waiting for you to get back.

> (**NOAH** *retrieves her sunglasses from the floor.*)

RÓISÍN. Ms. It's Ms. now, but she knows that. We've been having some tea, I've been having some tea. Noah didn't want any but he's been very gracious with his time.

BRENDA. He doesn't like tea.

RÓISÍN. Just look at you, you look wonderful.

BRENDA. I'm sorry, do we know each other?

RÓISÍN. I'm sorry, what?

BRENDA. I'm Brenda Hendriks.

RÓISÍN. Yes, and I'm Róisín Danner.

BRENDA. That's, what an unusual, that's a beautiful name.

RÓISÍN. Thank you. So I'm me, you're you and he's Noah. Apparently your son and all grown up. So we're all who we are. And I'm a bit shocked because I don't think I've ever heard you stutter over a sentence before in my life.

BRENDA. Are you sure we know each other? I'm having trouble placing [your...]

RÓISÍN. [Now don't] do that, I know you remember me.

BRENDA. All right.

RÓISÍN. I know I must be more memorable than that. Noah, all things considered and given our short time together, wouldn't you say I'm relatively memorable?

NOAH. Sure.

BRENDA. Noah.

NOAH. What?

RÓISÍN. You've seen me at my very worst, or at my worst then. Certainly I've seen worse since. How can you not, oh, is it because I'm calling you Brenda? Would your memory turn over a bit if I called you Connie instead?

BRENDA. There's no need to do that.

RÓISÍN. When I knew your mother, she was Connie. I didn't want to say anything to you about it in case she showed up here and I somehow had the wrong house. Wouldn't that have been embarrassing? But I had a feeling, a reliable feeling this time, and here she is. Finally. After so long.

NOAH. Connie?

RÓISÍN. That's right.

BRENDA. It's my middle name.

NOAH. Your middle name is Lynn.

RÓISÍN. Connie used to live next door to us.

NOAH. When did you live in Boston?

RÓISÍN. North of Boston. Next door to my husband and I, just the smallest strip of yard between us. Practically on top of each other, isn't that right, Connie?

BRENDA. Yes, yes, and it's Brenda.

RÓISÍN. Brenda. Yes. It's hard to just start thinking of a person as someone else all of the sudden. Even after this long, I know you can understand that.

BRENDA. Of course. And of course I remember you, Róisín. It's been such a, I don't know where my head is today. We're dealing with a bit of a "situation" regarding Noah's scholastic future [and I'm…]

RÓISÍN. [Yes, he] recounted a bit of it. Vandalism, such a shame. And I told him as much.

NOAH. Connie from Boston?

BRENDA. Clearly there's an explanation, Noah. And I will happily give it to you when we don't have company.

RÓISÍN. No need to be shy on my account, Connie.

BRENDA. Brenda.

RÓISÍN. Absolutely.

BRENDA. I am so sorry you had to sit here and wait. Noah, while sharing tales of your destructive exploits, did you offer Róisín something to drink?

> (**RÓISÍN** *moves back to sit at the table and lifts her mug to illustrate.*)

RÓISÍN. He did, the tea I mentioned; he's been an excellent host.

BRENDA. Has he?

NOAH. Yes.

RÓISÍN. I just said he has. We've been getting to know each other.

BRENDA. Have you?

RÓISÍN. Oh, these questions. But you and I? We have so much to catch up on. And you move around so much, what was the word, Noah? Nomadic. It's almost impossible to imagine I'm here. In fact, I'd be willing to bet you can't; you just cannot imagine what it's like for me to be sitting here with you right now.

BRENDA. It's certainly a surprise.

NOAH. She just showed up at the door.

BRENDA. I didn't see a car?

RÓISÍN. So I'll just have to keep reminding myself you're not Connie anymore. Brenda. Brenda Hendriks. Is that your husband's last name? Robert?

*(***BRENDA*** gives ***NOAH*** a cautious look.)*

BRENDA. You know about Robert?

RÓISÍN. Yes.

BRENDA. No, I didn't take his last name.

RÓISÍN. Am I doing it again, Noah, am I asking too many questions? Help me out here, I feel like I might be.

NOAH. It was my father's last name.

BRENDA. Noah?

*(He turns to face ***BRENDA***. His back is to the table where ***RÓISÍN*** sits.)*

NOAH. Yep?

BRENDA. Don't say *"yep."* And we discussed you taking a shower and actually putting yourself together today, didn't we? But look at you now.

*(***RÓISÍN*** uses a single finger to slowly, quietly slide her mug along towards the edge of the*

table. Her focus is on this task even when she interjects.)

NOAH. Well, Mrs. Danner got [here…]

RÓISÍN. [Ms.]

NOAH. Ms. Danner got here right after you left and I haven't [really…]

BRENDA. [I'm sure she's] just as eager as I am for you to make yourself presentable.

(He moves closer to her and tries to keep his voice down.)

NOAH. Jesus, Mom. I'm doing you a favor entertaining your friend while you're not here and you want to criticize me because I didn't have time to hop in the shower? That's exacting, even by your…

*(He is interrupted as the mug falls over the edge of the table and hits the floor with a splash of liquid. **BRENDA** and **NOAH** are startled.)*

RÓISÍN. Oh no, I'm sorry. I wasn't paying attention [and I just…]

BRENDA. [It's no] problem. Noah, go and grab a hand towel from the laundry room.

*(He exits. **BRENDA** speaks quickly in a hushed voice, the urgency amplified.)*

What are you doing here?

RÓISÍN. Looking for you. And clearly you didn't want to be found, why [is that?]

BRENDA. [Whatever you're] going to do, don't do it in front of Noah.

RÓISÍN. I'm perplexed, why would you think I'm here to do [something?]

BRENDA. [I won't play that] game with you.

RÓISÍN. I'm just thrilled that you suddenly seem to remember [me now.]

BRENDA. [What do you] want?

> (**RÓISÍN** *leans in and suddenly, for an instant, becomes a razor sharp dagger.*)

RÓISÍN. Any business I have is with you, Connie. If you're sending him away, do it quickly.

BRENDA. My name is Brenda.

> (**NOAH** *comes back with several hand towels and begins to clean up the spill. The women cover well.*)

NOAH. I'll get it. Did you get any on you, Ms. Danner?

RÓISÍN. Thankfully no. I only managed to make a mess of the floor.

NOAH. No mess, there you go. All clean.

> (**BRENDA** *retrieves the truck keys from her purse.*)

BRENDA. Noah, give me those.

NOAH. The dirty towels?

BRENDA. I'll finish cleaning up, I almost forgot that I need you to take the truck out to check on one of the turbines.

> (*He hands her the towels as she places the truck keys in his hand.*)

NOAH. Right now?

BRENDA. Turbine 7 isn't turning and from the drive it looks like it might even be leaning a bit. Go and take a look.

NOAH. I don't even know anything about them, what am I [supposed to…?]

BRENDA. [You don't have] to have a degree in mechanical engineering, just look it over at the base and see if there's any damage. If you spot anything unusual, we'll call it in to the company, this is not complicated.

NOAH. All right.

> (*He begins to leave.*)

BRENDA. And fill the truck up with gas. It's running low.

NOAH. Can I have some money for that?

BRENDA. You have money.

NOAH. No, I don't.

BRENDA. Use your tuition.

NOAH. Nice talking to you, Ms. Danner.

RÓISÍN. Yes it was.

NOAH. Play nice, Mom.

> *(He disappears out the front door.* **BRENDA** *exhales deeply, crosses to the other side of the room and sets down the towels. She turns to face* **RÓISÍN.** *They look at each other for a long while. Then…)*

BRENDA. You look well.

RÓISÍN. As do you.

BRENDA. Fit, bright. Thinner than I remember.

RÓISÍN. It has been some time.

BRENDA. That's true. It's my experience that people tend to go in the other direction as they age though.

RÓISÍN. Well, it's easy enough. I don't eat anymore. Anything really.

BRENDA. Anything?

RÓISÍN. Is that concern in your voice?

BRENDA. It just doesn't sound healthy.

RÓISÍN. Oh, it's not. But you'd be just amazed what a person can accomplish with just a little bit of purpose and an abundance of time.

BRENDA. Would I?

RÓISÍN. God, these little questions.

BRENDA. Well, we have to start somewhere.

RÓISÍN. By catching up? With pleasantries?

BRENDA. Yes.

RÓISÍN. Okay. Is that my son?

> *(Pause.)*

BRENDA. Róisín, I realize that we knew each other during a very difficult time in your life and I really did [my best to help...]

RÓISÍN. [That's the most] damning understatement of facts that I've ever, hmm, but not the point. Although your memory seems to be returning at an exponential rate.

BRENDA. I remember how devastated you were.

RÓISÍN. Perfect.

BRENDA. I remember trying everything I could to comfort you.

RÓISÍN. Comfort?

BRENDA. Is that too general?

RÓISÍN. I will not indulge your, I will not be deterred. I remember well your fondness for banter, for games, but I'm asking a very direct question: is that my son?

BRENDA. I don't know what this is, but that is ridiculous.

RÓISÍN. Answer me.

BRENDA. I did.

RÓISÍN. No, you didn't, you said a bunch of other things. Is that my son?

BRENDA. No.

RÓISÍN. No, he wouldn't be now. Not after all of this time.

BRENDA. He's not your son.

RÓISÍN. Just the right age.

BRENDA. The right age for what?

RÓISÍN. The age that my son would be now, isn't he?

BRENDA. Don't be [ridiculous.]

RÓISÍN. [If he hadn't] been taken out of his crib in the dead of night by some horrible, awful, [calculating...]

BRENDA. [He's my] son.

RÓISÍN. Repeating that over and over doesn't make [it true.]

BRENDA. [Is this why] you came? Get out [of my house.]

RÓISÍN. [How can you] even try to, just look at him; he even looks like me.

BRENDA. That's not true, he [doesn't.]

RÓISÍN. [It must make] you panic to [see it.]

BRENDA. [It doesn't] do anything of [the sort.]

RÓISÍN. [His skin, that] pale skin, just [like mine.]

BRENDA. [He just] doesn't like [the sun.]

RÓISÍN. [His hair. And] those eyes, so light, I never [even…]

BRENDA. [He doesn't] look anything [like you.]

RÓISÍN. [Ha! It's just so] painfully [obvious.]

BRENDA. [In every way] that matters he's mine!

RÓISÍN. Oh! Oh, I should be more specific, shouldn't I? You've no doubt calcified further into your word games with age, games that were never as cute as you thought, Connie, or as endearing and often something akin to justified lying, isn't that right? So I'll do that for you then, I'll be more specific: did that used to be my son? He's been dead to me for two decades, Connie. I'm not here for him, although finding him here with you did have an unexpected impact. The answer's not going to have any sway on what happens between us so tell me. Is that my son? Is that Ben?! Is that my Ben?! I already know, how could [I not know?]

BRENDA. [Róisín, stop] [this.]

RÓISÍN. [He was] standing right there looking like his father and humming the same goddamn song I used to sing to him as a baby, Connie, [the same…]

BRENDA. [Stop calling] me that! That's not [who I am.]

RÓISÍN. [Is that my] son!?!

BRENDA. Yes!

> (Pause. **RÓISÍN** *is momentarily shocked, but she fights through it. She begins to open and clench her fists involuntarily.*)

A long time ago.

RÓISÍN. And you took him.

BRENDA. And I left.

RÓISÍN. No, no, say you took him, say that.

BRENDA. I took him, yes.

RÓISÍN. From me.

BRENDA. Yes.

> *(Suddenly there is a thud on the roof of the house causing **BRENDA** to jump. It's followed by a few large scraping sounds, almost like large steps, something finding a footing. **RÓISÍN**, with no acknowledgment of the noises, exhales from somewhere deep inside and wipes the tears from her eyes. She rubs her fingers together with a bit of wonder, examining them.)*

RÓISÍN. I didn't know I could still cry.

BRENDA. What was that?

RÓISÍN. Actual tears.

BRENDA. What was that sound?

RÓISÍN. What sound?

BRENDA. You're telling me you didn't [hear that?]

RÓISÍN. [Frankly,] Connie, I'm more than a bit surprised you haven't fallen down apologizing yet.

BRENDA. Róisín, I know how it must seem [to you, but...]

RÓISÍN. [That's what] comes next. An apology.

BRENDA. I won't.

RÓISÍN. Oh no?

BRENDA. I will not.

RÓISÍN. Huh, well that is a pretty clear indicator that you don't understand what's happening here, the finality of this encounter.

BRENDA. Finality?

RÓISÍN. You hear me when I say these things, stop repeating them back as questions, stop trying to make me clarify, I'm not being at all cryptic. Finality. Finality.

BRENDA. I hear you.

RÓISÍN. Good.

BRENDA. And I've dreaded this, the possibility [of this.]

RÓISÍN. [You have] no idea.

BRENDA. But I won't apologize; I've done right by that boy.

RÓISÍN. So fucking [predictable.]

BRENDA. [And I'm] not sorry. I'm not. You were a wreck, after your husband left. You were a danger to that baby, you were a danger [to yourself.]

RÓISÍN. [My husband] left me, that's right, and I was young and all alone in that house, yes, with a baby. I had a right to be upset, to be sad. That's not the same thing [as not caring about...]

BRENDA. [You won't let me] rewrite my history, Róisín; don't you try to rewrite yours.

RÓISÍN. You rewrote my history, you did that.

BRENDA. You were depressed and not taking care of yourself and not taking care of him and out of your mind. That's very general, but you were generally out of your mind. And terrifying. When I would come over to clean up, to help out, you would muse about cutting his ear off and sending it to your husband, about leaving your new son in the middle of the street somewhere to get back at that man, about covering his face with a pillow to stop his constant crying, constant crying because he was hungry because you weren't [feeding him.]

RÓISÍN. [That's not] true, that's, people say things when they're, people say all kinds of things! That doesn't mean I would actually do any of it, not to my own son.

BRENDA. And the bruises.

RÓISÍN. Accidents.

BRENDA. And the screaming.

RÓISÍN. All babies cry.

BRENDA. All babies get broken arms?

RÓISÍN. They can.

BRENDA. All babies are so thin [that they...?]

RÓISÍN. [If you had such] enormous concern about my parenting you should have been more vocal, called the police, tried to do something about it.

BRENDA. The police? That's irrevocable, if they'd even believe me. And I didn't want that for you. I had a plan. So that it didn't have to be permanent. I had what I thought was a good plan.

RÓISÍN. Thrall me with this plan, please, thrall me with your grand scheme before I get the largest knife I can find, and take it to your face.

(*Pause.*)

Well?!

BRENDA. I wasn't going to keep him.

RÓISÍN. Look at him, he's had an entire life that I never [got to...]

BRENDA. [I just] needed to get him away from you until you got better.

RÓISÍN. Was he there in your house, the entire month? After he vanished, before you vanished, he was right next door?

BRENDA. No.

RÓISÍN. Where?

BRENDA. I left him with my mother.

RÓISÍN. Huh, your mother. That makes perfect sense. I don't mind telling you that makes so much sense that I'm thoroughly ashamed it didn't occur to me immediately, why didn't I easily put that together for myself? And then you left.

BRENDA. I left.

RÓISÍN. But until then, until it wouldn't be as patently obvious that you took my son, you stayed. And in a particularly sociopathic stroke of malice, you came over every day for a month to "comfort" me. To listen to me, to witness the fallout of what you'd done while making me tea, the same fucking tea I'm served at your table?

BRENDA. That's not what [I wanted.]

RÓISÍN. [To feel superior.] Maybe just [a little.]

BRENDA. [No, no it] wasn't like that.

RÓISÍN. Then what [was it like?]

BRENDA. [I weighed the] costs and made a decision.

RÓISÍN. You "decided" to be his mother.

BRENDA. I felt responsible. If I had to take him, I was going to make sure he had a better life, the best opportunities, [the chance to...]

RÓISÍN. [He was supposed] to have that with me.

BRENDA. You've come for this reckoning, but we both know you were in no state to ever give him what [he needed.]

RÓISÍN. [I don't know] anything of the sort and I don't give a damn about your theoretical assessment of the job I would have done as Ben's mother. If not for you, helpful you, always visiting you, lonely you in that house all by yourself because you never [had anyone.]

BRENDA. [That doesn't] have anything to [do with...]

RÓISÍN. [You were] jealous and you took him, you wanted him, you saw your opportunity and you took him. I know exactly what you wanted.

BRENDA. I wanted that boy to thrive.

RÓISÍN. No, you wanted that boy.

BRENDA. And I've done that, he's thriving, he's [becoming...]

RÓISÍN. [You raised] my son, my son, into a stranger and you liked it.

BRENDA. If that's what you think.

RÓISÍN. Think?!

BRENDA. I wouldn't expect [you to...]

RÓISÍN. [Who are] you?!

BRENDA. Róisín, you have to believe me when I say that I was destroyed to watch what you were going through and I tried [to make it...]

RÓISÍN. [You were the] cause of it!

BRENDA. I couldn't leave him there with you.

RÓISÍN. It wasn't your choice.

BRENDA. But I thought if I could just get your head clear, if I could just get you to see what you were doing to him, to yourself, then I could give him back. You remember, you said you remember, how I came every day to check on you. Because I wanted to give him back.

RÓISÍN. But you didn't give him back?

BRENDA. You never got better.

(Pause.)

RÓISÍN. I never...? I never got better?

BRENDA. You got worse.

RÓISÍN. You gave me a month.

BRENDA. I couldn't take the [chance.]

RÓISÍN. [Couldn't?]

BRENDA. Wouldn't.

RÓISÍN. Why can't you just admit you wanted him and you took him?

BRENDA. Someone had to do something [or else...]

RÓISÍN. [Someone] or you, someone [or you?!]

BRENDA. [I was] the someone there. And I knew I was, I knew in [my heart...]

RÓISÍN. [Say it, you] were what? Too alone, in need of purpose, wanting love, too [desperate...]

BRENDA. [I was what] that little boy needed; I could see it [in his face.]

RÓISÍN. [It's staggering.]

BRENDA. I knew I could do better [than...]

RÓISÍN. [It's] staggering!

BRENDA. I was better.

RÓISÍN. Do you hear yourself?! Who made you the judge and executor of his fate, my fate? And how could I ever get better when you took the only thing I had left in the [entire world?]

BRENDA. [He wasn't a] thing, he isn't [a thing.]

RÓISÍN. [Enough of] your patronizing semantic bullshit, the way you decide things for other people, it's enough, it's enough!

> *(She lunges at* **BRENDA***, striking her repeatedly. It is not decisive or controlled, it is unmoored.* **BRENDA** *does her best to defend herself, but* **RÓISÍN** *gets a grip on her throat as the women fall to the floor.)*
>
> *(As the women struggle, the sound of large groups of birds rises outside, wings flapping, calling, crying, a raucous thing. The intense, varied knocking on the door again and the deafening cries from above.* **BRENDA** *smacks* **RÓISÍN** *off of her for a moment and quickly crawls to the other side of the room.* **RÓISÍN** *sits up on her knees. The noise dies down again.)*
>
> *(Both women are exhausted, trying to catch their breaths. After a moment,* **RÓISÍN** *leans over and begins laughing, face down. The laughing turns into punctuated screams as she pounds her fist on the ground. After a few blows, she goes quiet.* **BRENDA** *is very still.)*

I never got better.

BRENDA. Your hands are like ice.

RÓISÍN. I never got better.

BRENDA. I don't know what else to say.

RÓISÍN. I never got better!! I never got better.

> *(Pause.)*

You used to ask me, ugh, I think I might be sick. You used to always ask me if I had any idea why all of this might be happening. During your "visits." And I always thought, you know, what an odd question. Because how could I know? How could anyone know that the only answer you wanted was, "Because I'm a bad mother"?

BRENDA. Róisín, even if that was unfair, I can't go back now and change [any of it]

RÓISÍN. [How is] your mother?

BRENDA. What?

RÓISÍN. I remember her from when she would come to visit. She was always so nice to Ben when we would see her getting into the car or out in the front yard. She would always give him a smile and he would smile back, even though he was just a baby. For a long time I had forgotten about her, but then one morning…

(*She snaps her fingers.*)

Just like that. "Connie's mother was always so kind." And always so generous to Ben, so complimentary. Both of you so covetous.

BRENDA. She was just being nice.

RÓISÍN. Is that what she was doing? When she was hiding my son, taking care of a baby that she clearly must have recognized as mine? She was being nice?

BRENDA. She helped me because I begged her to help me, to help Ben.

(**RÓISÍN** *cringes at this as she manages to get back to her feet.*)

RÓISÍN. So how is she?

BRENDA. She's, she was well the last time [we spoke.]

RÓISÍN. [Was she?]

BRENDA. Yes.

RÓISÍN. Well when I saw her, she wasn't well at all.

(*Pause.*)

BRENDA. When did you see her?

RÓISÍN. What if I told you she was incredibly difficult to track down? Not as difficult as you, but when I say years I know you'll believe me. And what if I told you that when I saw her, she looked just the same? Well, in fairness, she was tied to a chair with a belt and I think that I already mentioned to you my fondness for large knives. She was willing to tell me anything I wanted to know about you, your whereabouts, your new name, your son. She aged well.

BRENDA. You didn't do that.

RÓISÍN. I wonder, was she being nice then, too? Telling me everything? And after I got that everything I needed, I wanted to untie her for you Connie, I really did. I wanted to bandage her up, help her. But I told myself that I would leave her there until you decided to apologize. But unfortunately you never did, Connie. I never got better and you never apologized and your poor mother and all of this.

> (**BRENDA** *uses a nearby piece of furniture to hoist herself back to her feet.*)

BRENDA. What did you do?

RÓISÍN. What did you do?

BRENDA. Is she, is she [all right?]

RÓISÍN. [It's so difficult] when people begin to disrupt your family, isn't it? Oh, do you think Noah will be back soon?

BRENDA. If you hurt my mother, [I will...]

RÓISÍN. [I hurt] your mother. I did that; it's done.

> (**BRENDA** *scrambles to the nearby phone and frantically begins to dial.*)

Oh yes, please call her.

BRENDA. You didn't do anything to her, how would you even find her?

RÓISÍN. I found you.

> (**BRENDA** *suddenly looks at the receiver in horror.*)

BRENDA. Mom?

RÓISÍN. Busy signal? Oh, I might have left it off the hook. Hard to fathom, isn't it? There's nothing you can do about it right now, so accept it. Accept that you can't do anything. And what would you do? Would you call the police? You haven't yet. Oh no, wait, you can't. Because you're a kidnapping traitor and you care more about saving yourself than turning me in. Do you want me to call the police?

(Pause.)

I'll call them for you.

(**RÓISÍN** *reaches out for the phone.* **BRENDA** *hangs it up quickly.)*

No. That's right. Neither of us wants the police. That's not what you want for me right now, is it? And that's not the kind of justice I have in mind for you.

BRENDA. *(Quietly.)* Did you kill my mother?

RÓISÍN. Let's just wait for Noah to get back?

BRENDA. Did you kill my mother?

RÓISÍN. We'll see what he thinks about [all of this.]

BRENDA. [Did you?!]

RÓISÍN. Well I certainly didn't do her any favors, Connie. You're fond of understatement, isn't that right? And I'm not really in a good place to be doing any favors for any of your loved ones. So, as I'm sure it just slices you up to imagine, I won't be doing any favors for Noah.

BRENDA. Oh, god. Why would you tell him any of this? It will crush him.

RÓISÍN. Whoever Noah is, he's not Ben. You killed whoever my son would have been and replaced him with that unfamiliar albeit polite young man and I don't really care what it does to him as long as it hurts you.

BRENDA. You do still care, you can try to hide it, even if you're this monster now, [even if...]

RÓISÍN. [Oh, I am] a monster.

BRENDA. But you didn't expect him to be here. That's what you meant earlier, isn't it? You never thought you would see him. And now that you have [you can't...]

RÓISÍN. [And now that] I have it makes eviscerating you even sweeter.

BRENDA. I can see that it hurts you.

RÓISÍN. Everything hurts me!!!

BRENDA. He won't believe you.

RÓISÍN. Shouldn't be too long now.

BRENDA. He won't.

RÓISÍN. Isn't this fun?

BRENDA. I should... I should kill you.

RÓISÍN. Now that's refreshing.

BRENDA. Leave now or I will make you [regret ever...]

(**RÓISÍN** *laughs at her and it is cruel.*)

RÓISÍN. [Ah, I suspect you've] been making that calculation since you walked in the door and saw me with "your son."

BRENDA. I will do it, Róisín. To keep you from hurting him, from hurting anyone [else, I will absolutely...]

RÓISÍN. [Now, I'm truly] fascinated by this; how would you do it? In order to spare others the hurt, how would you kill me?

BRENDA. I don't [think...]

RÓISÍN. [In what] manner would you take my life?

BRENDA. My bare hands if that's what [it takes.]

RÓISÍN. [Your bare] hands? Not a knife? Not shotgun to take off half my face? Not a rope around the neck with a pull until you hear that awful cracking noise and everything [goes limp?]

BRENDA. [I don't] need anything except [my hands...]

RÓISÍN. [You can't] kill me.

BRENDA. Yes I can, I will.

RÓISÍN. All right, well do your best, Connie, but you're too late. I died seven years ago.

BRENDA. What [are you...?]

(**RÓISÍN** *flies into a rage, her fists clenching and releasing involuntarily again with barely controlled fury.*)

RÓISÍN. [That's right,] dead. Dead! You can't kill me because I'm already dead. And I don't mean that figuratively, emotionally, I don't mean from the weight of the grief. I mean dead: numb hands, icy skin, no heartbeat, not a sound. You know, after you left me there with nothing, no husband, no son, no comfort at all, it only took me a few months to begin to suspect. You also suddenly vanished. And so soon after my boy, how peculiar? I couldn't find you, not a trace. No one could find you. And it suddenly became clear to me what must have happened. Not clear, but it began to make sense. Why would someone just disappear? Someone who had so often expressed deep concern for my son, for something she knew nothing about?!

> (**RÓISÍN** *picks up a framed picture and squeezes it so tightly the wood begins to crack. Then she smashes it on the ground.*)

And after thirteen years of mourning my missing son, hating you and wishing for any kind of ending, I finally reached a limit and drowned myself. In the bathtub. Which takes a hell of a lot of conviction, let me tell you.

BRENDA. Oh my god.

RÓISÍN. But I did it, I held myself under until I swallowed half the water in that tub and my eyes felt like they would spill out, burst open. But just look, I'm still here. And I've tried since then Connie, trust me. I hung myself, I cut myself open, I drank bleach, and I'm still here. Dead and still here.

> (*She looks at her own hands and starts laughing. It's deeply unsettling.*)

Because I'm not done, you see? Because instead of my son, I raised a bird, a wounded little bird that grew into a starving terror, starving for vengeance, a gigantic fucking beast that's sitting on your roof right now, so heavy, biding his time, getting impatient, can you hear him? And he won't let me finally be done until I finish this. Finish with you.

BRENDA. You really are insane.

> (**RÓISÍN**'s *laughing becomes more intense, almost maniacal.*)

RÓISÍN. Would that be better?

BRENDA. You want me to believe there's a giant bird outside [that you...]

RÓISÍN. [I raised] him and he loves me. And he wants me to finish [this.]

BRENDA. [The lengths] to which you'll go to [try and...]

RÓISÍN. [I'm so tired,] Connie, but he's making me [finish this.]

BRENDA. [This is] lunacy!

RÓISÍN. Because it sounds impossible? Because [it sounds...?]

BRENDA. [Yes!]

> (**RÓISÍN** *walks over, grabs her clutch, and produces a large knife.* **BRENDA** *backs away.*)

RÓISÍN. Okay. Okay. All right, you see this?

BRENDA. Oh god.

RÓISÍN. Oh, now you're afraid? Why? You think I'm crazy and violent and possibly as vicious as you. You think I brought this to stab you mercilessly over and over? What if I simply have this handy? Maybe I brought it along just in case you couldn't wrap your myopic, self-important mind around the scale of all of this, the sheer magnitude of my hate, because, Connie, it is truly...boundless.

> (**RÓISÍN** *slowly stabs herself in the stomach or side with the knife with little to no reaction.* **BRENDA** *however screams. The woodpecker calls out from the roof as it moves around some more, getting a new footing. There is some blood as* **RÓISÍN** *pulls the now bloody knife out of her body.* **BRENDA** *makes a break for the door, but* **RÓISÍN** *gets in her way.*)

Not much blood. Honestly, I don't think there's much left.

BRENDA. This isn't real, this [isn't real.]

RÓISÍN. [It's real. And] now there is a ravenous woodpecker roughly the size of your house that does nothing but hate and hate and hate because that's all I ever gave it to eat. And that's impossible and ridiculous and insane!

> *(She approaches **BRENDA** and brandishes the large, bloody knife. Suddenly the flapping of enormous wings as the bird takes off from the roof.)*

But whether you believe it or not, he's up there getting more and more restless and I'm right here without a pulse and you will pay for how you've wronged me. He will bring this house down and when I tell you that neither of us will leave here today so you had best begin digesting the finality of it.

> *(The front door flies open, startling both women as **NOAH** rushes in. He slams the door and looks out a window. **RÓISÍN** hides the knife behind her back.)*

NOAH. Did you see that?

BRENDA. Oh God, Noah, we're, we're having a private conversation [and you...]

NOAH. [Mom,] turbine 7 isn't leaning, it's bent over like something slammed [into it.]

BRENDA. [Noah.]

NOAH. Like a car or, but higher up [than a car.]

BRENDA. [Noah!]

NOAH. And coming up the drive I saw something huge fly away [from the house.]

RÓISÍN. [Just think, he] used to fit right here.

> *(She holds out a cupped hand to **NOAH**.)*

NOAH. What?

RÓISÍN. So small, just like I [told you.]

NOAH. [Is that, are] you bleeding?

RÓISÍN. Not much.

BRENDA. I need you to go into town and get the police.

NOAH. What's going on?

RÓISÍN. How do you think you know that song I was [singing earlier?]

BRENDA. [Noah, go into] town and get the police for me, right now.

NOAH. Why? Can't you just [call them?]

RÓISÍN. [She wants you] to leave, have you ever noticed how pale your skin is?

NOAH. I just don't go in the sun [very often.]

BRENDA. [Noah, go.]

> *(She pushes him out the front door and closes it. She holds it closed as he tries to get back in, knocking and calling from outside.)*

NOAH. *(From offstage.)* [Mom!]

BRENDA. [Your issue] is with me and that thing, It's after [me, right?]

RÓISÍN. [Are you asking] me to show you [kindness after...?]

NOAH. *(From offstage.)* [Mom, what is] [going on?]

BRENDA. [Róisín, he has an] entire life to be [hurt! Please!]

RÓISÍN. [I don't] know if I [can, Connie.]

BRENDA. [Maybe I was] wrong, I was only doing what I thought was right, but you're right, I did want it, I did, so don't hurt him just to hurt me.

> *(**NOAH** forces his way back inside.)*

Just hurt me.

NOAH. Mom!

BRENDA. Noah, you have to take the truck back into town and [get the police.]

NOAH. [Are you insane?]

(**RÓISÍN** *crosses to* **NOAH**. *Keeping the knife hidden, she takes the slip of folded paper from her pocket. She quickly pushes it into his front pocket and then steps back a few feet, squeezing her fists. She closes her eyes tightly.*)

RÓISÍN. [Get him out] of here.

BRENDA. Bring them back here; you have to do that for [me now.]

NOAH. [Mom, I] don't [understand...]

RÓISÍN. [Make him] leave now, Connie, I can't bear this!

(**BRENDA** *pushes* **NOAH** *to the door. The thumping sound again on the roof, the agitated scraping noises. The sounds of birds noisily beginning to mass seeps in.* **NOAH** *looks up, but* **BRENDA** *keeps him moving. She opens the door to a chorus of birds scattering outside.*)

BRENDA. You don't have to understand, but you [do have to go.]

NOAH. [I can get her] out of here if [that's what...]

BRENDA. [I love you.] Go.

(*She pushes him out and slams the door. She turns to* **RÓISÍN** *who opens her eyes again. There are tears on her face, but she is not weeping. The birds are knocking against the walls and their flapping wings and calling become a shifting, restless bed of sound that can be heard inside.*)

Thank you.

(**RÓISÍN** *gasps for air and then steadies herself.*)

RÓISÍN. You're welcome.

BRENDA. He will go into town.

RÓISÍN. I'm sure he will.

BRENDA. He will bring the police back here.

RÓISÍN. I'm sure he will.

BRENDA. He is a good boy.

RÓISÍN. I'm sure that's true.

BRENDA. He will come back.

RÓISÍN. And he will find this house collapsed, piles of wood, nothing salvageable. Our bodies will be picked clean to the bone, and then what's left will be carried away.

BRENDA. All of it?

RÓISÍN. Carried away to heaven.

BRENDA. But Noah will be all right.

RÓISÍN. As far as you or I know.

BRENDA. Then it was worth it.

> (**RÓISÍN** *drops the bloody knife.*)

RÓISÍN. Oh Connie, that all depends on the heaven part, doesn't it?

> *(The birdcalls from outside grow even louder, the flapping wings. It is perhaps the sound of hundreds of birds now. Growing louder and louder. The thud on the roof deafening cries and scrapes, wood beginning to crack. The light from outside grows dimmer somehow and seems to writhe with motion.)*

BRENDA. I want to, I don't know how to say this to you.

RÓISÍN. I'm stunned.

BRENDA. Róisín, I am sorry how I hurt you. And how it made you this. I've tried in every way to live my life without, I never want to regret things, but I do regret what I did to you. I do. We were friends once.

RÓISÍN. I used to believe that, yes.

BRENDA. So even now, I want you to know that I mean it.

RÓISÍN. I do. And I so wish that was enough.

> *(The cry from the giant woodpecker on the roof rings out again. The light grows even*

dimmer as the mixing of the bird noises quickly swells to a deafening cacophony that swallows the stage.)

*(A dim light gently creeps downstage. **NOAH** is suddenly illuminated in a special standing alone off to the side across from the shadow screen wall of the living room. His hands are in his pockets. He wears a lightweight jacket.)*

(As he speaks, the screen wall begins to glow. Just the wall, leaving the rest of the living room dim and creating an eerie, isolated effect. The shadow images revealed on the wall are a few rolling hills with a line of wind turbines in the distance.)

(They slowly turn. It's lovely. Perhaps there is the gentle sound of the immense turbines in the distance.)

NOAH. When I got back to the house with the police that day, it was decimated, nothing but a pile of wreckage, a pile of all the things that used to be home. They brought in a rescue team to search and I just stood at the end of our drive with my back to the scene and watched the wind turbines turning on the hill. Oblivious. Quiet. They're very quiet, you can barely hear them at all.

The funeral was hard. That's not specific, she would tell me to be specific. The funeral was a herculean effort on my part to remain composed while lowering an empty box in the ground. No body. Not many friends to speak of, but somehow an abundance of flowers. So many flowers. Robert came back from Alaska and we negotiated a very mature parting of the ways. I didn't expect him to still be my father, but he loved her. I did watch him try to salvage her garden and felt more affection for the man than I ever had.

Afterwards, I went to stay with my grandmother. I was going to tell her all of it and just try not to care that the entire thing sounds crazy. But when I got to her house, she had her own story for me. One day she came home from dinner with her friends and someone had broken in, shattered all of the windows, torn things down, ripped wiring out of the walls, even the roof was damaged; the entire house was ransacked. But as far as she could tell, the only thing missing was her address book. And there were feathers. She found feathers everywhere.

I still don't know what happened the morning that strange woman showed up at our door. The piece of paper she pushed into my pocket? A note: "Woodpeckers are some of the only birds that knowingly steal other birds' eggs." How messed up is that? I just... I can't make myself throw it away.

The thing about my Mom, she only ever wanted the best for me. I don't have to know everything about her to believe that. Who really knows everything about their parents, I guess? But I still drive out here sometimes, away from the city lights. When night falls, I look at the stars, so clear and somehow closer, and I remember her teaching me about the constellations. How they hang in the night sky, where we all fit, the larger scope of things. About right and wrong.

> *(A shadow of a flock of birds flies by in the distance on the screen.)*

And I miss her. Every day.

> *(Some birds sound in the distance. As the lights fades, the sound of the wind turbines sweeps everything into darkness.)*

End of Play